ISS

Re

CC/MB/£4.95
7/12/84

For Tilia and Sylvie for being
so very patient with the tortoise
P.W.

For Glenn and Jonathan
C.C.

THE HARE
AND THE TORTOISE

Retold by Caroline Castle

Illustrated by Peter Weevers

HUTCHINSON
London Melbourne Sydney Auckland Johannesburg

Hare got out of bed one morning feeling so fit he leapt two feet in the air just for the pure joy of it.

'Never was a faster hare,' he said to himself as he preened his whiskers in the mirror.

He did his exercises and briskly brushed his teeth before setting off on his morning run.

Once outside, Hare took a deep breath and set off at a fast pace. He ran like the wind, jumping hedges and leaping streams with ease. Three times he went round the forest and he wasn't the least bit tired at the end of it.

On his way back, Hare met Badger busily sweeping the path to his set.
'Morning, Badger,' said Hare.
'Morning, Hare,' replied Badger. 'Been out for a run?'
'As I do *every* morning,' said Hare in a very superior voice. 'I'm extremely fit.' And he stood on his hands to prove his point. Badger only yawned.
'Show off,' he said to himself when Hare was gone.

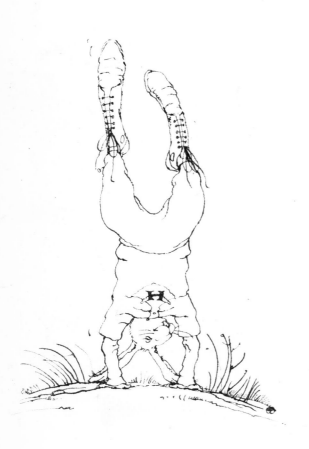

That same morning Tortoise was sitting up in bed writing his book *Great Tortoises of the World*. He'd already got to page 749 and was just checking the birthdate of Tortonimus the Third when his tummy rumbled.

'Ah,' he scratched his head. 'I've forgotten breakfast again.'

Then he looked out of the window. It was a fine day. 'I think I'll go out for a picnic,' he said to himself.

He filled his hamper full of good food, and took two bottles of his favourite fizzy lettuce juice.

Tortoise was just settling down by the river with his book when Hare came along. Now there was something about Tortoise that annoyed Hare immensely; but he didn't know quite what it was. Perhaps it was the way he never got up before lunchtime, or the way he ambled along not caring what time of day it was, or the way he smiled that silly, contented smile, as if he knew some wonderful secret.

'What time do you call this to get up?' Hare asked Tortoise scornfully. 'You'll never get anywhere just sitting around reading books.'

'Beats spending your life running round in circles,' replied Tortoise, raising a sleepy eye. 'Where, exactly, does that get you?'

'If you must know,' said Hare, 'I'm the fastest hare hereabouts.'

'Good for you,' muttered Tortoise. 'Yet for all your speed, even I could beat you in one of your hare-brained races.'

Hare laughed and laughed. He laughed so hard that his sides ached, and so loudly that Badger and Mole came to see what all the fuss was about. 'Tortoise says he can beat me in a race,' said Hare, barely able to speak through his laughter. 'ME! The fastest hare in the countryside!'

'Well,' said Badger. 'Why don't you take him on?'

And so he did.

A day was set for the race. Badger was selling tickets for a penny each. Mole was trying to mark out the track, watched by a curious sparrow who wondered what on earth was going on, because however hard Mole tried, he just couldn't seem to get his molehills to come up in the right places.

Frog was in charge of announcing the race.
He travelled the countryside proclaiming in a
very loud voice:

'Oyez! Oyez!
The race between the Hare
and the Tortoise will be on
Sunday afternoon at three o'clock.
Come early to avoid disappointment.
Tickets one penny each.'

When the great day arrived there was an atmosphere of excitement and festivity. Frog was selling balloons: a red one if you supported Hare and a green one if you supported Tortoise. Squirrel arrived and set up a tea tent with tables and chairs outside. Even Fox, who never came to anything, turned up at the last minute. Hare was the first to arrive for the race, cheered on by a group of hares from the running club who had come along for a good laugh. Just as the race was due to begin, Tortoise ambled up in his usual leisurely fashion and sat down to drink a cup of tea at Squirrel's tent before making his way to the starting line. Badger dropped his handkerchief and they were off. Caps and scarves waved frantically as the animals cheered on their favourites. It wasn't long before Hare was so far in front that when he looked back Tortoise wasn't even in sight.

Hare began to slow down.
'What a ridiculous race,' he said to a group of spectators
sitting on the bank. 'Why, it's beneath my dignity as a hare
even to take part in it!'
It was a lovely warm day with a clear blue sky and he decided
to sit down for a short rest. If
he waited all day, Tortoise
would never catch
him up.

The sweet smell
of summer drifted over him. The scents of honeysuckle and
rose, lavender and sweet pea wafted under his nose and soon
lulled him off to sleep.
Hare began to dream. He dreamt he was in the Fastest Hare Race.
He dreamt that all the great hares were there: Harrier Hare, Fast
Legs and Leaper among them, all the heroes of his youth. Hare
dreamt he led the race from the beginning and was soon so far in
front that he had time to look back and
see the others struggling behind.
He came in first to a great cheer
from the crowd, so loud
that he awoke almost
at once.

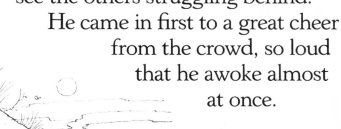

But the cheer wasn't for him. What Hare saw
when he opened his eyes was Tortoise
just about to cross the finishing line.
He leapt up and ran as fast as he could.

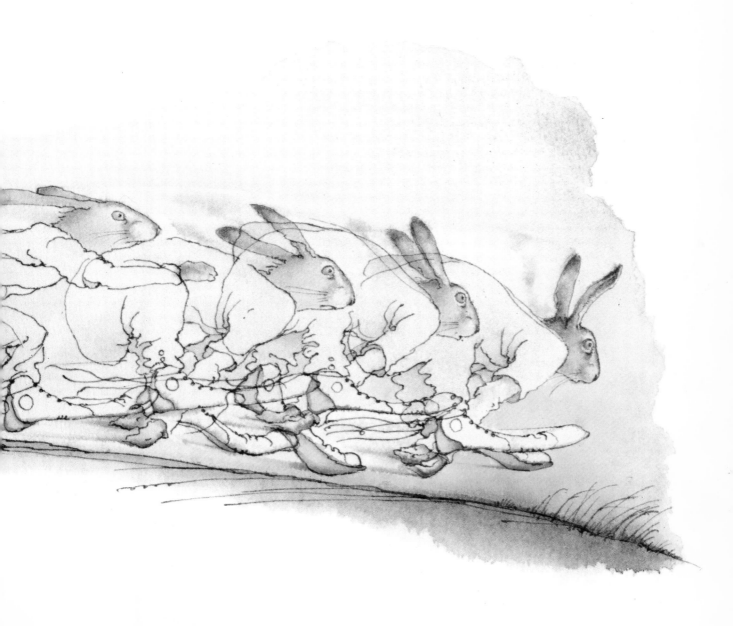

But it was no use. Tortoise had won.
'You beat me!' said Hare in amazement
'Yes,' replied Tortoise, and he smiled
his own special smile.
'By a hair's breadth, you might say.'

And he ambled off to write another page of his book.

THE END

Hutchinson Children's Books Ltd

An imprint of the Hutchinson Publishing Group

17–21 Conway Street, London W1P 6JD

Hutchinson Publishing Group (Australia) Pty Ltd
PO Box 496, 16–22 Church Street, Hawthorne, Melbourne,
Victoria 3122

Hutchinson Group (NZ) Ltd
32–34 View Road, PO Box 40–086, Glenfield, Auckland 10

Hutchinson Group (SA) Pty Ltd
PO Box 337, Bergvlei 2012, South Africa

First published 1984
Text © Caroline Castle 1984
Illustrations © Peter Weevers 1984

Set in Linotron Horley Old Style by Tradespools Limited

Printed in Great Britain by Jolly & Barber Ltd
and bound by Hunter & Foulis Ltd

British Library Cataloguing in Publication Data
Castle, Caroline
    The hare and the tortoise.
    I. Title   II. Weevers, Peter
    823'.914 [J]   PZ8.2

ISBN 0 09 156750 5